Lightning Strikes Twice

Two unusual pets with something in common. Firstly there's Yob, struck by a blow which muddles his thinking and makes him a back-to-front pet, once called Boy but now only responding to Yob.

Then there's Fred struck by a sudden bolt from the blue which leaves him charged with energy and transformed into Lightning Fred, the fastest tortoise in the world.

Dick King-Smith

LIGHTNING STRIKES TWICE

Illustrated by Abigail Pizer

MAMMOTH

The stories in this book were previously published as
Lightning Fred, first published 1985 by William Heinemann Ltd
Text copyright © 1985 Dick King-Smith
and *Yob*, first published 1986 by William Heinemann Ltd
Text copyright © 1986 Dick King-Smith
This edition first published 1991 by Mammoth
an imprint of Mandarin Paperbacks
Michelin House, 81 Fulham Road, London SW3 6RB

Mandarin is an imprint of the Octopus Publishing Group,
a division of Reed International Books Limited

This edition copyright © 1991 Dick King-Smith
Illustrations copyright © 1991 Abigail Pizer

ISBN 0 7497 0733 X

A CIP catalogue record for this title
is available from the British Library

Printed in Great Britain
by Cox & Wyman Ltd, Reading, Berkshire

Contents

Yob   7

Lightning Fred   36

Yob

'THERE'S A BODY!' yelled Joanna
suddenly. 'By the side of the road — just
back there — oh, stop, Dad, do!'

Her father did as he was told. He

stuck his head out of the window of the Land-Rover and peered back through the teeming rain that was driving in across the moors from the sea.

'Sheep, I expect, Jo,' he said. 'Got hit by a car, probably. They lose a lot like that in this part of the world.'

'It didn't look woolly,' Joanna said. 'It might have been a person.' She shivered. 'Oh please, Dad, let's go back and see.'

'All right, chicken, don't get yourself in a state,' said her father. He put the Land-Rover in reverse. 'Like I said, it'll be an old sheep. Tell me when to stop, I can't see a thing in all this rain.'

'Bit further,' said Joanna, head stuck through the side-window.

'Bit further. Stop! Oh, Dad!'

'What is it?'

'It's a dog!'

'Dead?'

'I don't know. It's not moving. Oh, Dad, please have a look.'

Her father sighed and got out. He walked around the back of the Land-

Rover and bent, hands on knees, to look at the large limp shape that lay, with the raindrops bouncing off it, at the edge of the moorland road.

'Dead as a button, I should think,' he shouted above the noise of the storm. 'Great big chap too — whoever hit him will have a good old dent in their car, I should think.'

'Is there a name and address on his collar?'

'Half a tick. No address, just his name. "Boy". Poor old Boy. Not much we can do for him, I'm afraid.'

But when Joanna's father got back into the Land-Rover one look at his daughter's face told him all he needed to know. Mr Best was a farmer and well used to dealing with all kinds of awkward animals — high-spirited horses, cross-grained pigs and hot-eyed bulls. But always, when he saw his eight-year-old daughter's chin set firm and her eyes blaze, he knew that there was more trouble ahead than he could handle.

'There's nothing we can do, Jo,' he said again. 'We'd better get on. We've had a long day at the Show and we've got a long way to go yet before we're home.'

'We can't . . . just . . . leave him here.'

'But look, chicken, we haven't even any idea who he belongs to.'

'Dad!'

A couple of hours later the Land-Rover turned off a main road, down a lane, and into the yard of the Bests' farm. Joanna's mother came out to greet them.

'Did you have a good day at the Show?' she said. 'What was the weather like?'

'Show was all right,' said her husband. 'As for the weather, it was enough to make a parson swear. It rained cats and . . . it was very wet.'

'Jo? Have you had a nice time?'

'We found a dog,' said Joanna in a voice of deepest gloom, 'that had been run over. He's called Boy . . . he was called Boy. He's in the back. Dad has promised to bury him . . . in the orchard . . . under the pear-tree. I'm going to make a cross and put his name on it,' and she stumped off, head bowed in mourning.

Mr Best let down the tail-gate of the Land-Rover.

'Look at the thing,' he said to his wife. 'It's the size of a month-old Friesian calf.'

'Couldn't you have just left it?'

'She wouldn't let me,' said her husband.

He took hold of the hindlegs to pull the body out.

'Funny,' he said. 'He still feels quite warm,' and then they saw, in the clear sunlight of a now fine evening, the gentle rise and fall of the dog's ribs.

'Jo!' shouted Mr Best. 'Jo!' and as she came running back, 'Look!'

Slowly, as though waking from a deep sleep, the dog called Boy opened his eyes.

'Well, there's nothing terribly serious wrong with him,' said the vet.

It was later that evening, and the dog had undergone a thorough examination. He had submitted to it without protest, perhaps realising, as animals do, that someone was trying to help him. He did not wag his tail but simply stood quite still with a faraway look in his eyes.

'He doesn't answer to his name,' said Mr Best. 'Boy! Boy! See, he doesn't even look at me.'

'Shock, I expect,' said the vet. 'He's obviously been concussed. No bones broken, but he's had one heck of a bang on the head. Has he eaten anything?'

'No. We've offered him food, but it was funny, he sat and looked at it but he wouldn't touch it, almost as though we'd told him not to.'

'I'm sure he wanted it,' Joanna said. 'He was dribbling.'

'Oh well,' said the vet, 'he'll eat when he's hungry enough. A good night's sleep won't do him any harm. He seems to have had quite a day what with being knocked out cold in the middle of Exmoor in a storm, and then coming to and finding himself in a strange place with strange people. He's a fine big fellow, isn't he?'

'What sort of a dog is he, d'you think?' Joanna asked.

'Well, he's not pure bred, that's for sure. If you're asking me for an educated guess I should say he's Irish Wolfhound cross Labrador. Got his size from his father and that black satiny coat from his mum. No chance of entering him in Shows and adding to all those silver cups your father's won for his cattle. But then you'll try to find his owners, I imagine?'

'I've already contacted the police,' said Mr Best.

'What if they can't trace them?'

'Well I suppose we'll have to find him a good home.'

'He's got a good home,' said Joanna very quietly.

'Now look, chicken . . .'

'Dad!'

'We'll see.'

'Well now, I must be off,' said the vet. 'Let me know how he goes on.' He patted the dog's back. 'Finished with you, old chap. You can take the weight off your feet. Sit!' The dog remained standing. The only movement he made was to turn his head and look at the vet with what Joanna thought was a puzzled expression.

'Sit!' said the vet again, with no result.

'Funny,' said Mr Best. 'You'd have thought he'd have been trained to do that at least. After all, he's not a puppy.'

'No,' said the vet, picking up his bag and turning to leave the room, 'I should say he's at least two years old. Why he doesn't know a simple command like that I simply cannot under*stand*.'

At the sound of the last part of this final word the dog immediately sat down. Only Joanna saw this, for the two men had walked out.

'You funny old Boy,' she said. 'Now at last you've decided to sit.' No sooner had she spoken that last word than the dog stood up again, looking at her to see if he had done the right thing. But when without thinking she said 'Good dog,' he looked distinctly unhappy. He hung his head and his long tail went between his legs.

'What's the matter?' said Joanna. 'There's no need to look so miserable. You haven't done anything bad.'

Once again this final word produced a very odd result. Up came Boy's head and out came his tail and began to wag, slowly. A ridiculous idea suddenly occurred to Joanna. 'He's had one heck of a bang on the head,' the vet had said. Bangs on the head did funny things to people, didn't they? Might not bangs on the head do funny things to dogs?

Just suppose, she thought . . . could it possibly be that . . . well, there's only one way to find out.

'Bad,' she said again, softly.

The tail wagged faster.

'Bad,' said Joanna in a louder voice. 'Bad! Bad!! You *bad* dog!!' and the big black animal wagged his tail like mad and whined with pleasure and licked her hand.

The truth burst upon Joanna.

'Stand!' she commanded, and Boy sat.

'Sit!' she ordered, and he stood up again.

16

'*Bad dog!*' said Joanna severely, and a moment after that her father came back into the room to see his daughter kneeling with her arms round the dog's neck, having her face thoroughly washed, while Boy's whole body curved to and fro in an ecstasy of tail-wagging.

'Oh, Dad!' cried Joanna. 'I've found out what's wrong . . . he's got everything back to front in his mind . . . it must have been that bang on the head . . . just watch!'

She got to her feet.

'Stand!' she told Boy and he sat down.

She ran to the door.

'Come!' she called and he stayed exactly where he was.

Then she ran out of the room, and came back with a big bowl of food. She put it on the floor at the far side of the room as man and dog looked on. They both stayed quite still, but one began to dribble.

'Now then, Dad,' said Joanna, 'watch this,' and she turned to the dog.

'Stay!' she said and he came to her.

'Sit,' she said and he stood beside her.

She pointed at the bowl.

'Eat it up!' she said.

Still he stood, looking up at her, waiting for the next command. Joanna grinned at her father.

'Now then,' she said to Boy, 'don't you touch that food, d'you hear me? Don't you dare touch it,' and before the words were out of her mouth the meat was in his, as he gulped and swallowed, gulped

and swallowed, and finally polished the bowl with his tongue.

'So that's why he wouldn't eat before!' said Mr Best, softly. 'Because we kept telling him "Eat it up, eat it up, there's a good dog".'

'Which means "Don't touch that, you bad dog" now,' said Joanna. 'Everything's opposite.'

'Only one thing I don't understand, chicken,' said her father. 'Why won't he answer to his name? Boy! Boy! See, he doesn't even look at me.'

'Like I told you, Dad,' said Joanna. 'Everything's opposite now. You're still calling him by his old name, the name he answered to before his accident. We can't use that any more.'

She went to the door and she called 'Yob! Stay!'

And Yob came running.

Next morning Mr Best sat stirring his tea. His wife was washing up, his daughter had gone to the village school, and, with a couple of hours of the day's work already done, he felt like sitting quietly with his third cup and thinking. Usually he thought about problems, like a sick cow or a broken-down tractor or if it would rain (when he wanted it to) or keep dry (when he wanted it to). Now he was thinking about Yob.

'Stay,' he said, and the dog came. 'Up, Yob!'

With a grunt of relief the dog settled at his feet.

'Finished your tea, Bill?' asked Mrs Best, coming in.

'Mm. I was just thinking.'

'About the dog? Whether to keep him?'

'Jo's very keen to.'

'Well then that's that,' said his wife, with a smile. 'And anyway he's a lovely . . .'

'Careful!'

'I mean, he's a horrible nasty bad dog!'

Yob's tail thumped happily.

'And I suppose,' she said, 'we'll all get used to doing everything backwards.' She took an uneaten slice of toast from the rack and dropped it in front of Yob's nose.

'Don't touch!' she said, and he ate it.

'What's worrying me, Mary,' said her husband, 'is that he's very likely to be claimed. A dog like that . . . been well-fed . . . name on his collar . . . been trained even if he's got it all scrambled now . . . someone's bound to be looking for him. They'll take him back and that's going to break Jo's heart.'

At that moment the phone rang.

'A chap's coming about four o'clock,' said Mr Best after he'd replaced the receiver.

'Oh dear. Jo will be home from school by then.'

'What's the matter?' said Joanna when she saw her parents' gloomy faces. 'It's not Yob? He's not ill?'

'No,' said her father, 'but he's been traced, Jo. A man's coming to collect him, shortly.'

'Oh,' said Joanna.

'Look, chicken, we'll get you a puppy. You're old enough for a dog of your own.'

'I don't want a puppy,' said Joanna. 'I just want Yob.'

Yob's tail banged the floor at the sound of his name and then came another sound, of a car. There was a knock on the front door.

Half of Joanna wanted to rush away so as not to set eyes on this person, not to see him take the dog away, not to have to say goodbye. The other half, the curious half, made her hide behind the curtains.

Peeping round, she saw her parents showing a man into the room, a short fat man with a very red face.

'Ah, there you are, Boy,' he said in a loud voice. 'Boy! Boy?'

Yob, who was sitting on the hearth-rug, did not even look round.

'He doesn't seem to know you,' said Mr Best. 'Have you had him since he was a puppy?'

'No. I bought him quite recently from people going abroad. I wanted a big animal — as a guard dog, you know. I've a great many valuable things in my house.'

Bet you haven't got masses of silver

cups like Dad has, thought Joanna behind the curtains, and you look horrid and you sound horrid and I wish I hadn't stayed to see you.

'Of course we've only been looking after him for twenty-four hours,' said Mr Best, 'but we find he doesn't always do exactly as he's told.'

'He'll do as I tell him,' said the red-faced man. 'Get up, Boy!' Yob lay down.

'Come!' said the man in an even louder voice.

The dog stayed put.

'What the devil's the matter with him?' said the red-faced man.

Mr Best caught his wife's eye and then said, 'Do what you're told, there's a good dog.'

At these last words Yob looked the picture of misery.

'Did I understand you to say,' said the red-faced man slowly, 'that he'd had a bang on the head?'

'A heck of a bang.'

'He doesn't look well to me.'

'No, he doesn't, does he?'

'Something very wrong with him.'

'So it seems.'

'Well see here, Mr Best, I don't believe in beating about the bush. A dog that behaves as strangely as that is no use to me.' Behind the red-faced man the curtains moved a fraction.

'He's not a bit of good to me,' he went on (and at 'good' Yob cringed even further away), 'so you do what you like with him. Waste of my time coming all this way. I'll be off.'

'Jo! Jo! Where are you?' called her father when the man had gone.

'Here,' said Joanna, coming out, 'and you said I was old enough for a dog of my own.'

As time passed, the Bests grew used to living with an animal to whom 'Yes' meant 'No'.

Sometimes indeed they fell into the same way of thinking themselves, and for example a breakfast-time conversation might run like this:

Mr B: Don't pass the marmalade, Jo.

Joanna (passing it): Shan't.

Mrs B (absently): Don't speak so *politely* to your father.

Mr B: When I said 'marmalade', I meant 'honey'.

Joanna: Can I get up? I've started.

Mrs B: Of course not (Joanna gets down.)

But on the whole they reserved back-to-front language for the dog Yob. There were two things they learned not to say in his hearing. One was 'Be quiet', which made him bark like mad, and the other was 'Down!'

Yob's response to this word was to leap up and, standing on his hindlegs, place his forefeet on the speaker's shoulders (luckily they were Mr Best's), and attempt to lick him to death.

'He really is the friendliest dog, isn't he, Bill?' said Mrs Best, one day when they'd had Yob for a while.

'Yes. Fat lot of use he'd have been to that chap as a guard dog.'

'I suppose he might have been fierce before his accident changed things. D'you suppose he was running away from home when he got hit?'

'I bet he was,' said Joanna. 'I bet he was trying to find his first owners. Trying to get away from that man. I didn't like him one bit. Horrible beast!' and at these last words Yob came to her squirming with pleasure.

'What d'you suppose he'd do to a burglar, Dad?' she said.

'Kiss him.'

A couple of weeks later, a burglar came.

Burglars come in all shapes and sizes, and this one was small and thin and always posed as a businessman. He would stay at a country hotel or pub and liked to chat with the locals. He was interested in old houses, he told them. Were there any stately homes in the district? Or Georgian mansions? Or Queen Anne manor-houses? Or even an Elizabethan farmhouse? Thus he learned that the Bests lived in such a house, and that Bill Best had won many valuable silver cups and trophies with his pedigree dairy cows.

Well worth melting down, thought the burglar, and next day he drove straight to the Bests' farm and knocked on the door.

'I'm sorry to trouble you,' he said to Mrs Best when she opened it, 'but I've lost my way. I wonder if you could direct me to . . .', and he gave the name of a village a few miles away.

While she was talking, he noted (with pleasure) that the catch on the nearest window was a simple one to force and (with annoyance) that there was a very large black dog standing in the hall.

'What a big fellow!' he said. 'Is he friendly?'

Mrs Best laughed.

'My husband thinks,' she said, 'that if a burglar came, Yob would probably give him a kiss!'

That afternoon the burglar bought something in a butcher's shop. That evening he parked his car in an out-of-the-way spot not far from the farm, and prepared for action.

When the grandfather clock in the hall struck twelve for midnight (a noise through which the family, as always, slept, but which covered the sound of a carefully opened window), a figure slipped over the sill and stood listening.

The burglar was wearing a black track-suit. On his feet were black plimsolls, on his hands black leather gloves. Over his eyes was a black mask. In his left hand was a sack, in his right hand a torch. In his pocket was a pound of fresh pig's liver. In the liver was a powerful sleeping-pill.

Just my luck, thought the burglar

happily, as a great array of silver cups and silver bowls and even a silver model of a cow winked and sparkled at him in the beam of his torch.

At that moment there was a noise in the next room that sounded like a yawn, which it was.

Just my luck, thought the burglar sadly, as the torchlight shone on the large black figure standing in the connecting doorway.

'Hullo, Yob,' he said very softly.

Yob wagged gently at the sound of his name.

Dropping the sack, the burglar drew

the lump of meat from his pocket and tossed it on the floor. The delicious smell of the pig's liver filled Yob's nostrils, and he stood and stared at this nice man, hoping for the right command.

'Eat it up,' whispered the burglar.

Yob stood, waiting.

'Eat it up,' whispered the burglar again. 'Eat it up, there's a good boy!'

At these words Yob backed unhappily away, banged into a small table, and tipped it over.

'Be quiet!' hissed the burglar, and at this Yob began to bark.

'Stop it!' said the burglar, so Yob kept on, loudly enough now to wake the dead, let alone the Bests.

'You *horrible* dog!' the burglar snarled. 'Why don't you pipe *down*!'

When Mr Best appeared, shotgun in hand, and turned on the lights, he saw before him on the floor a lump of raw meat.

Beyond that lay Yob, and under Yob lay a black-clad figure that struggled feebly under a shower of kisses which increased to a slobbery storm as the burglar cried, 'Oh stop it, stop it, you beastly dog!'

When the police had come and taken the burglar away, the Bests looked fondly at Yob.

'Isn't he wicked!' said Joanna.

'Dreadful!' said her mother.

Her father looked at the congealing liver.

'I think you deserve a big reward,' he said to Yob, 'but that will do for a start. Don't touch it!'

They watched as the hero of the night gulped it down. Then suddenly his eyes began to glaze and his legs to buckle, until finally, like a great tree falling, he crashed to the floor and lay still.

'That meat was laced with dope,' said the vet later. 'He'll be out cold for a while. Last time I saw him I seem to remember saying that a good night's sleep wouldn't do him any harm. That's what he's going to get.'

'We could all do with some,' said Mr Best. 'Go on, chicken, up you go.'

Joanna tried hard to stay awake but suddenly, it seemed, it was broad daylight. She jumped out of bed and rushed downstairs. Yob still lay exactly as he had fallen. For an instant he looked as dead as when first she had set eyes on him, but then she heard him snoring. Joanna sat on the floor beside him.

There's only one way to wake you, she thought, and she lifted the flap of his ear.

'Go to sleep!' she said.

Contrary as ever, the dog opened his eyes.

'Bad-morning, Yob!' said Joanna happily.

Lightning Fred

DIGBY WAS NINE and tubby and Dot
was seven and short in the leg. They
were not fast runners. This didn't bother
Dot, but Digby's secret ambition had
always been to win a race at the School
Sports. One year, when there had been
chicken-pox, he had come in third. But
then there had only been two other boys
running.

'Only a week to Sports Day and this
year I'll be in the Boys' Under-Ten 100
metres,' thought Digby, red-faced and
puffing, not from thinking it but from
running back from school to get home
before the threat of a thunderstorm.

'Quick!' their mother had called from
the cottage door as they stumbled up the
garden path, forgetting to shut the gate,

and quick, thought Digby, is what I wish I was.

Now he knelt beside his sister on the sofa and looked out at the rain bucketing down.

'Phoo!' he said as the lightning flashed. 'Glad we're out of that.'

Dot let out a sudden wail. 'Fred!' she cried. 'Where's Fred?'

At that moment the lawn outside was suddenly lit up and thunder banged almost immediately.

'There he is,' said Digby. 'By the sundial. Hope it doesn't act as a lightning conductor.'

'Oh, Dig, don't say that! Oh, Mum, can I get him in?'

'No, certainly not,' said their mother. 'Tortoises are quite safe in thunderstorms. He'll just pull his head and legs in and let the rain bounce off his shell,' and she went out of the room. The next instant there came a huge clap of thunder, right above the cottage roof it seemed, and a brilliant crackling, hissing

zigzag that almost blinded them. Automatically, they put their hands before their eyes.

When they looked again, they could see that the tortoise was lying tipped upon his back. He seemed to steam slightly in the pouring rain.

'He must have a proper grave,' sobbed Dot.

The storm had gone, and the children stood by the motionless shape of Fred. Digby had tipped him right side up with the toe of his wellie, and they could actually see where the bolt of lightning had hit him. They had painted their name and address and telephone number on his shell, but now most of the red paint had disappeared under a crescent-shaped brown scorch-mark that left only the phone number showing.

Digby bent down to touch this mark with a finger, and then suddenly leapt very high in the air.

Dot stopped crying in amazement.

'Dig!' she said. 'I didn't know you could jump that high!'

'Nor did I', said Digby. 'It gave me a sort of shock, touching that burn-mark. Not a nasty shock, just sort of exciting. It made me feel, well, powerful. You try it.'

'No, no. I don't want to touch him. We must bury him. Will you make a hole?'

'All right.'

'And we ought to write something. Like they have on gravestones. Can you think something up, Dig?'

Digby thought.

'How about this?' he said.

    'Here lies our tortoise.

    His name is Fred.

    He was alive.

    But now he's dead.'

'That's lovely,' said Dot in a choked voice. She blew her nose hard.

'You go and write that out on a bit of wood or something,' said Digby, 'while I get the grave ready. Under the weeping willow tree.'

A couple of minutes later, Dot came running back to the sundial, carrying her handiwork. There was no sign of Fred, so she ran to the willow tree where Digby stood beside an empty hole.

'Why didn't you bring him?' he said.

'I thought you'd fetched him,' she replied.

They stared at each other. Then they began to grin like gargoyles.

'He wasn't dead!'

'He's walked away!'

'Good old Fred!'

'Let's tell Mum!'

They ran indoors. 'Mum! Mum, Fred's not dead!'

'Oh, good, I am glad.'

'He's wandered off somewhere. We're going to look for him.'

'I expect he's shell-shocked. Anyway, while you're looking, I'm just going to walk up to the post-box with these letters. Shan't be long.'

Just after she had gone, the phone rang. Digby went indoors to answer it. He came back to Dot, looking thoughtful.

'Who was it, Dig?'

'A lady ringing up to say she'd found a tortoise.

'Who? Where?'

'Someone who lives in Hatch Norton.' Hatch Norton was the next village.

'But that's two miles away!'

'Yes.'

41

'And Fred's only been gone ten minutes.'

'Yes.'

Dot struggled to do the sum in her head.

'He must have been going at least twelve miles an hour,' said Digby.

'But that's stupid. It can't be Fred, it must be another tortoise.'

'With our phone number on its back? And a crescent-shaped mark on the shell, the lady said.'

They stared at each other.

'But how shall we get him back?'

'The lady said she was coming this way this evening and she'd drop him off. I gave her our address.'

Just then their mother came in at the garden gate. 'Have you found where Fred's got to?' she said.

'Yes,' said Digby.

'Thank goodness for that,' said his mother. 'Otherwise I should have thought there was something very strange going on. The funniest thing's

just happened. As I was walking up the lane to the post-box, I saw a bicycle lying on the grass verge and then a pair of legs sticking out of the ditch. It was old Mr Fosse, you know, the road-mender, and he was lying there as white as a sheet. I helped him out, and you'll never believe the crazy story he told me.'

'What was it?' Dot said.

'He said — he must have been drinking or else he's gone quite potty — he said that he'd been cycling along when

43

suddenly he was passed by an animal.'

'What sort of animal?' Digby said.

'A tortoise!' his mother said with a shriek of laughter. 'A tortoise, if you please. One really shouldn't laugh at the poor old man. It rushed past him at tremendous speed, and gave him such a shock that he fell off his bike. Talk about seeing pink elephants!'

'Which direction was it going, Mum?' asked Digby.

'Towards Hatch Norton, Mr Fosse said. It was all in the poor old chap's imagination. I mean, imagine Fred dashing past a cyclist. It takes him half a day to cross the lawn.'

At that moment the children heard the distant sound of a car.

'We're going to play out in the lane for a bit, Mum,' Digby said.

Outside, the children ran a little way down the lane and stared expectantly at the approaching car. It slowed at the sight of them and then stopped, and a lady wound down the window.

'Are you the children who've lost a tortoise?' she said.

'Yes,' said Digby. 'It's very kind of you to bring him back.'

'Well, I should think you must have given up all hope of seeing him again ages ago,' she said with a smile. 'It must take about a year for a tortoise to travel two miles! Sensible for you to have painted your number on him. Incidentally, how did he get that funny crescent-shaped mark on his shell?'

'He had an accident,' Digby said quickly. 'Did you touch it? The mark, I mean.'

'No, I certainly did not. I'm sorry, but I'm afraid I'm not a tortoise lover. They rather give me the creeps with their snaky heads. In fact I actually had to put on a pair of rubber gloves before I could bring myself to pick him up. Anyway, here he is,' and she handed a cardboard box out of the car window.

When they had thanked her and the car had driven away up the lane, Digby carried the box into the garden.

'Make sure the gate's shut this time, Dot,' he said.

In a far corner of the garden, hidden from view, they put the box on the ground and opened it.

'He *looks* just the same as ever,' said Dot.

'Except for that crescent-shaped mark,' said Digby.

'Dig, you're not going to touch it again, are you?'

'Look, I just want to try something,' Digby said. 'D'you think I could lift that big log there with one hand?'

'Don't be silly, Dig, of course you couldn't. It's much too heavy. You couldn't even move it.'

Digby took hold of the log with both hands. He could not budge it an inch.

'You're right,' he said. He took a deep breath, and bending over the box, he pressed his finger to Fred's burn-mark. Then he turned, picked up the log one-handed, and raised it high above his head. Slowly, easily, he lowered it down again.

'Oh!' gasped Dot. 'How could you . . . ?' I don't understand.'

'I'm sure it's electricity,' Digby said.

'How do you mean?'

'When that bolt of lightning hit Fred, it must have discharged its electricity into him. That's why he could whizz past old Mr Fosse, and that's why he got to Hatch Norton in ten minutes. Good job that lady did put on her rubber gloves, because Fred's actually become a generator! He's not just Fred any more — he's Lightning Fred! All you've got to do is to touch that mark and Lightning Fred charges your batteries, makes you able to do things that you couldn't possibly do ordinarily, like jump high or lift heavy weights.'

'Or,' said Dot thoughtfully, 'run fast, like he can?'

'Yes!' said Digby. 'Oh, yes, Dot! Of course! Gosh! Are you thinking what I'm thinking?'

'Yes! Sports Day. Oh, Dig!'

They stared at each other.

'How long before your . . . your batteries run down again, Dig?'

Digby tried again to lift the log, first with one hand, then with two. He could not budge it.

'Not long, Dot. But long enough.'

After supper they found the cardboard box empty, with a tortoise-shaped hole in one side, slightly charred around its edges.

'Oh, no!' said Dot. 'Now where's Lightning Fred gone?'

'Look!' said Digby, gripping his sister by the arm. 'Look over there!'

Something round and low that seemed to glow in the gathering dusk was rushing across the lawn.

'What a sprinter he'd make!' breathed Digby as the tortoise shot into the shrubbery.

'What a sprinter you'll make, Dig!' said Dot.

First thing next morning, the children found Lightning Fred in the shrubbery, just where he had disappeared at speed the night before. He did not look at all electrified, just the same old Fred, but the old Fred had not had that crescent-shaped burn-mark on his shell.

'After school,' said Digby, 'we'll take him somewhere secret, where no one can see us.'

'And you'll charge your batteries?'

'Yes.'

'And run like the wind!'

'Hope so.'

Before they left home Digby said to his mother, 'You will keep the garden gate shut, won't you?'

'Of course. I always do. Why, specially?'

'Oh, just in case Light . . . just in case Fred should get out.'

His mother laughed. 'He wouldn't get very far if he did get out, would he?'

'Oh, I don't know.'

'Anyway, off you both go to school

now or you'll be late. Anything special happening today?'

'There's a practice for the Sports,' Digby said.

The village school was a small one, and there were only nine others of his age in the line-up that afternoon when it came to the time for a trial run of the Boys' Under-Ten 100 metres.

Unfortunately, though Digby's dreams the previous night had all been of racing to victory, he trailed in so far last that the winner had come jogging back past him towards the start line before he'd even reached the finish.

'Keep going, Dig,' he said as he passed.

'Good old Dig!' the spectators cried as they watched his clumsy shambling efforts. Try as he would, his arms seemed to wave about, his body to wobble, and his legs, instead of going straight forward and back like pistons, had apparently to make a circling movement to get round his bottom.

Red-faced, puffing, Digby grinned as he always grinned in defeat. Before, that grin had been to hide his disappointment, but now there was another, happier, reason for it.

'Well tried, Digby,' his teacher said, and to the others, 'we can't all be hares, you know, and anyway don't forget the fable — the tortoise won in the end.'

'I'll do better on the day,' Digby said. 'I'm going into training.' All the boys fell about laughing.

You just wait, Digby thought.

When school finished Digby and Dot hurried home as fast as they could. Would Lightning Fred have escaped again? Would he still be supercharged? He hadn't, and he was, as they could see as soon as they came into the garden.

The tortoise was grazing on the lawn, but, startled by the click of the gate, he took off at top speed, dashing off like a small runaway tank to disappear into the shrubbery. Digby bent over him.

'You're not going to charge your bat-

teries yet, are you, Dig?' Dot said. 'Mum might see.'

'No. I just want to make sure that it's only touching the burn-mark that does it and that anywhere else is O.K. After all, we're going to have to carry him around with us. On Sports Day *you'll* have to carry him.'

'Oh, no!'

'It'll be all right, Dot, I'm certain. Look, I'll try and then you can.'

Digby reached down and scratched the top of Lightning Fred's head, then his leathery old neck, then, in turn, each leg, and finally he put his hand on the shell, the front of it, the back, the sides, everywhere except the cresent-shaped mark.

'There, you see, I didn't feel anything. It's only that one place. Go on, you try now, Dot.'

'Oh, Dig, must I?'

'Yes.'

Gingerly, making a dreadful face, Dot began to copy what her brother had done.

'See, I told you it's all right. Pick him up.'

'Oh, no! Suppose he runs away with me?'

'He can't run if his feet are off the ground. Go on, Dot, you've got to. Otherwise the plan won't work.'

'I can't. I'm frightened.'

Digby played his trump card. 'Oh, all right then. If you can't help me I shall just trail in last in the race. As usual.'

The thought of this was too much for Dot. Biting her lip, she grasped Lightning Fred with both hands, one on each side of his shell, and lifted him up.

'I did it!' she said. The tortoise stared owlishly at her.

'Come on,' said Digby. 'We'll go up the lane to that long narrow field by the wood. I'll carry him.'

When they reached the field, Digby gave the tortoise carefully back to Dot and marked out a rough 100 metres with two sticks, counting aloud and taking large clumsy steps.

'If only he can win that race!' said Dot softly to Lightning Fred. 'It's got to work. It must work.'

Once Digby had measured out his track, he came back to the starting stick. They stared at each other.

'Good luck, Dig,' said Dot.

Digby looked round but the only other living thing to be seen was an old horse peering over a gate at the far end.

'Right. Here goes,' he said.

He turned to face the finish.

'Hold him out, Dot,' he said, and when she obeyed he put a finger firmly on the crescent-shaped burn-mark.

Watching him intently, Dot saw a shiver run through him. Then after a little pause, so suddenly that it made her jump, Digby was off, tearing along the field faster than she had ever seen any boy run, faster than any boy ever *had* run. There was no change in his style — his arms still waved wildly about, his body still wobbled, his legs still swung around his fat bottom — but everything waved or wobbled or swung five times as fast as usual. It was like a speeded-up film.

Almost before Dot could draw breath, Digby was past the finishing stick, travelling at such speed that he only just managed to pull up before the far hedge. Horrified, the old horse galloped away. Digby turned and began to walk back, punching both fists in the air with excitement.

'Dig! Dig!' yelled Dot. 'Try running back. See if it's still working.'

'All right!' shouted Digby, but when he set off again, it was at the old plodding pace.

'It doesn't last long,' he panted when he reached his sister.

'But long enough! Gosh, you were *flying* along, Dig. I don't know how you kept your balance.'

'It was so easy,' said Digby. 'I just felt as light as a feather, and yet so strong! It was marvellous!'

'Are you going to have another go?'

'No. I'd love to but I don't think I'd better. We know it works for running now, and for long enough for me to win the 100 metres. But what we don't know is how long I can go on recharging from Lightning Fred without using up his power. We must save it for Sports Day.'

On the morning of Sports Day Dot carried her shoe bag to school. She had left her trainers and P.E. kit in her locker, and the bag, which she hung up in the changing room, contained only Lightning Fred. Somehow the morning, and lunch (Digby could hardly eat a thing) seemed to drag by, but at last the moment came.

The infants had had their little races, the long jumpers and the high jumpers had performed, and Dot's part in the Sports was over. She had come fourth out of seven in the Girls' Under-Eight 70 metres, of which she was quite proud, considering the shortness of her legs.

Now she asked her teacher, 'Can I go to the toilet, please?'

Once indoors she quickly took the shoe bag from its hook, opened it, checked on the tortoise, and popped a clean handkerchief inside.

Everyone was watching the girls of Digby's age racing, and Dot made her way carefully to the starting-line and stood near to one end of it. Within a few minutes the call came, 'Boys' Under-Ten 100 metres!' and the ten competitors began to line up, Digby making sure he was closest to his sister.

'Are you ready?' called the teacher who was starting the races.

'Just a minute, sir,' said Digby quickly. 'Can I blow my nose?'

'It's supposed to be you that's running, Digby — not your nose.'

'Oh, please, my sister's got a hanky.'

'Hurry up, then.'

Quickly Dot pushed the shoe bag towards him, its mouth open. Quickly he pretended to use the handkerchief while with the first finger of his other hand he found and pressed the magic mark. Then he was back in the line-up, tensed, quivering, ready.

'One . . . Two . . . Three . . .' but at 'Three' several of the keenest made a false start.

'Come back!' called the teacher. 'Come on back, you lot.'

The seconds ticked by, as the offenders trailed back, maddeningly slowly.

'Dig! Dig!' hissed Dot through the noise of the spectators. 'It'll be too late!'

They stared at each other.

'Sir!' cried Digby desperately. 'I need to blow my nose again!'

'Don't be silly, Digby, I can't wait for you and your nose. Now then, One . . . Two . . . Three . . . GO!'

To the watchers it seemed that Digby was still fumbling about for his handker-chief as the other nine sped away. They had covered twenty metres before he took his hand from the shoe bag again, but the shouts of glee that arose at the sight of old Digby — of all people — still fiddling about when the race had started were suddenly stilled as he shot off in pursuit. Only Dot's shout of 'Come on, Dig!' broke the awestruck silence.

At thirty metres he had cut their lead to half, at forty he was level, at fifty well ahead, and from then on all that the other runners saw was a disappearing blur of arms and legs as he hurtled away from them like a greyhound from a bunch of Pekingese. By the time the fastest of his opponents had reached the finishing-line, Digby was almost a further hundred metres ahead, braking hard to avoid hitting the railings at the far end of the playing-fields.

Then he turned and walked slowly, clumsily, back to the rest of the school, the remains of the burst finishing-tape wrapped round his proudly heaving chest, the usual grin on his red face. How they cheered!

Later Digby just couldn't recall the

rest of the Sports Day. Still to come were all the events for the oldest children — their running races, the obstacle race, the egg-and-spoon, the Marathon (twice round the playing-fields) — but all he could remember afterwards was the look of amazement on the face of the head-master as, amidst a storm of applause, he presented him with the cup for the Boys' Under-Ten 100 metres.

'Well done, Digby!' he said. 'I don't know what got into you!'

'It was quite a shock, sir,' Digby said.

When they reached home (Dot was allowed to hold the little cup, while Digby carried the shoe bag), they put Lightning Fred out on the lawn, and dashed indoors.

'Mum! Mum!' yelled Dot. 'Dig won his race!' and she showed her the trophy.

'Digby!' cried his mother. 'How super! I didn't know you were a fast runner.' She gave him a hug. 'To be truthful,' she said, smiling, 'I didn't think you were much faster than old Fred!'

Digby smiled too. 'I'm not!' he said.

They all looked out of the window and there on the grass stood the tortoise, motionless at the spot where the children had placed him. And as they watched, they saw him, very cautiously, stick out his snaky old head, and then, very very slowly, reach out first with one foot and then another, and start to crawl at a snail's pace across the lawn.

'At least I wasn't,' said Digby. 'Even today.'

'But now it looks as if you are again,' said Dot.

They stared at each other.

Then they suddenly burst out laughing.